The Very Best EASTER BUNNY

Written by Ann Braybrooks
Cover illustration by DRi Artworks
Interior illustrations by Josie Yee

 A GOLDEN BOOK • NEW YORK

Golden Books Publishing Company, Inc., New York, New York 10106

Early one Easter, as Pooh and his friends were decorating eggs, Rabbit hurried over.

"Sorry, but I can't play the Easter Bunny this year," he announced. "I have to plant my garden. Here, Pooh, you do it."

Pooh knew that someone had to play
the Easter Bunny or there wouldn't be an
Easter egg hunt, so he tried on the costume.

"Oh, help and bother," he said, struggling with the zipper. "It doesn't seem to fit."

Finally, Pooh was dressed. "You don't look like the Easter Bunny, Pooh," Roo said anxiously.

"I suppose not," said Pooh. "But maybe I can act like him. Watch."

Pooh gave his biggest smile, then scrunched
down and tried to hop. But the bunny feet were
too floppy, and Pooh plopped to the ground.

"Let me try it," Tigger insisted. "Hopping is what Tiggers do best."

Tigger stepped into the costume and pulled it up. "Oops," he said. "It ripped."

Tigger wasn't the kind to let a small thing get him down. "Ta-ta for now!" he cried happily. Then he hopped—or, rather, bounced—high into the air.

Tigger hopped and hopped, higher and higher. Suddenly he came crashing down on the table where the Easter eggs were waiting. A few eggs bounced off the table and cracked.

"Hopping is not what Tiggers do best after all,"
said Tigger as he picked up the eggs. "Maybe *you*
should play the Easter Bunny, Kanga."

Kanga held up the costume. "It won't fit me, Tigger, dear."

"What about Eeyore?" Roo asked hopefully.

"Don't look at me," said Eeyore. "I'm the wrong shape. Naturally."

"Don't look at me, either," Owl chimed in.
"My Uncle Aesop dressed up as a rabbit once—or
was it a hare?—and then a tortoise—"

Piglet coughed. "I'd play the Easter Bunny," he said, "but I'm too little."

"Me, too," said Roo, wiping away a tear. "I guess we can't have an Easter egg hunt this year."

"I'll think of something," Pooh said. He scratched his head. He hummed a little hum. Finally, he said, "I must make Rabbit believe that he is the only one who can play the Easter Bunny."

"Do hurry," urged Kanga.

Rabbit was in his garden. He was so busy planting seeds he didn't hear Pooh cry, "Rabbit! Ahem! Rabbit!"

"Rabbit does have a lot to do," Pooh said to himself. "If we want him to help us, then we should help him."

Pooh hurried back to his friends and explained his plan. The whole group trooped back to Rabbit's, eager to help.

In no time, the garden was planted.
"That's a relief," Rabbit told the others. "Now
I have time to play the Easter Bunny."

Everyone returned to Pooh's house. Rabbit put on his Easter Bunny costume. He noticed the broken zipper and the rip, but he was in such a good mood he didn't complain.

"I'll hide the eggs before you can say 'rutabaga!'"
he cried. "And, remember, no peeking!"

"Hurray for Rabbit!" everyone cried, as Rabbit headed into the woods. "Hurray for the one and only Easter Bunny in the Hundred-Acre Wood!" They all went into the house and shut the door. And only Tigger tried to peek.